D1504965

CHOP, SIMMER, SEASON

MENU

Basket of Fresh Baked Breads
Top Notch Minestrone
Garden Greens
Grilled Trout with Harvest Vegetables

Strawberry Layer Cake
Cherry Chocolate Cupcakes
Apricot Tart

ALEXA BRANDENBERG

HARCOURT BRACE & COMPANY
San Diego   New York   London

For Stacey, Douglas, Toby, and Jordan
and in memory of Wayne Lovelace

Requests for permission to make copies of any part of the work
should be mailed to: Permissions Department, Harcourt Brace & Company,
6277 Sea Harbor Drive, Orlando, Florida 32887-6777.

Library of Congress Cataloging-in-Publication Data
Brandenberg, Alexa.
Chop, simmer, season/Alexa Brandenberg
[author and illustrator].
p.   cm.
Summary: The chefs at the Top Notch Restaurant prepare dinner.
ISBN 0-15-200973-6
[1. Cookery—Fiction.   2. Restaurants—Fiction.]   I. Title.
PZ7.B73625Ch   1997
[E]—dc20   96-5279

First edition
F E D C B A

Printed in Singapore

The illustrations in this book were done in gouache on 400-lb. Strathmore watercolor paper.
The display type was set in Tekton Bold and the text type was set in Leawood Medium
by Harcourt Brace & Company Photocomposition Center, San Diego, California.
Color separations by United Graphic Pte Ltd., Singapore
Printed and bound by Tien Wah Press, Singapore
This book was printed on Nymolla Matte Art paper.
Production supervision by Stanley Redfern
Designed by Judythe Sieck

Top Notch
Restaurant

Yawn, Stretch

Measure

Sift

Mix

Knead

Rise

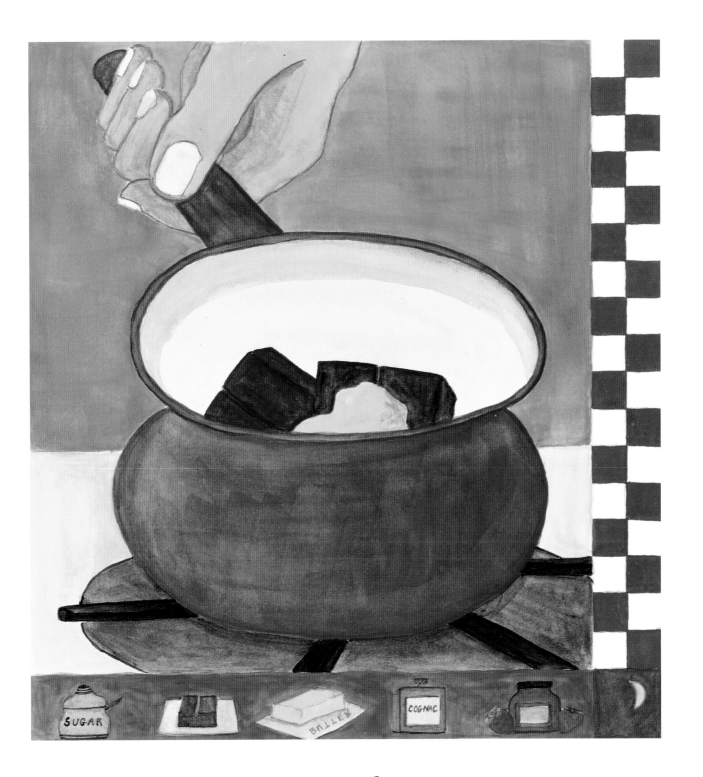

Melt

Beat

Bake

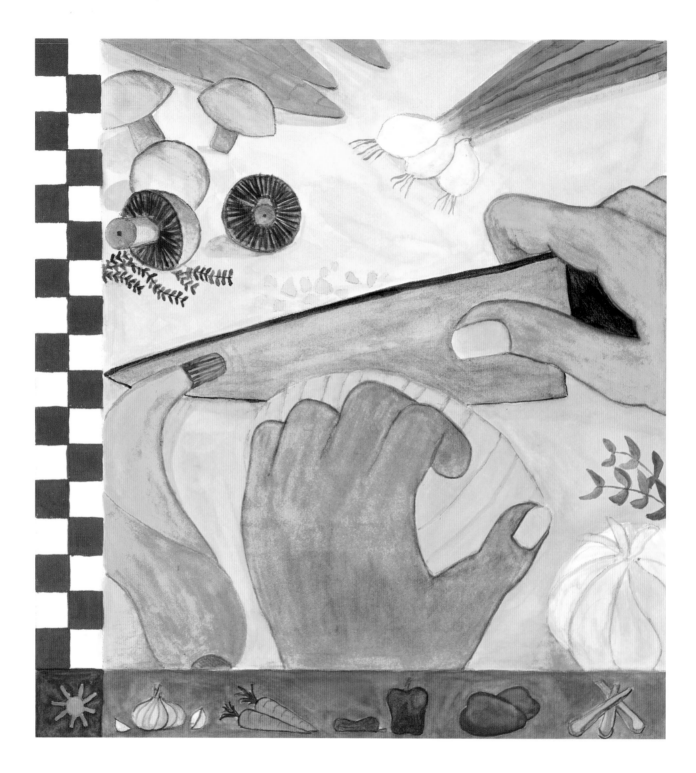

Chop

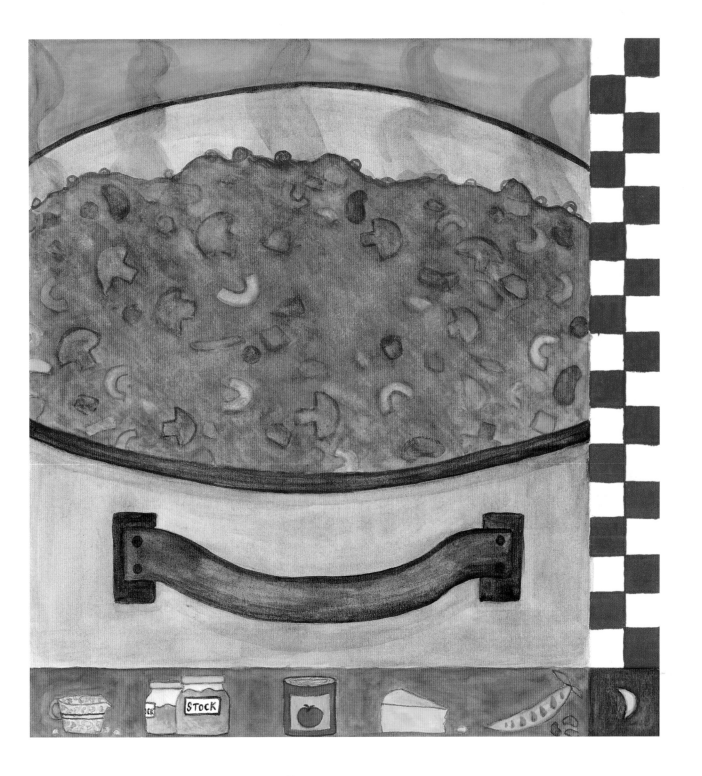

Simmer

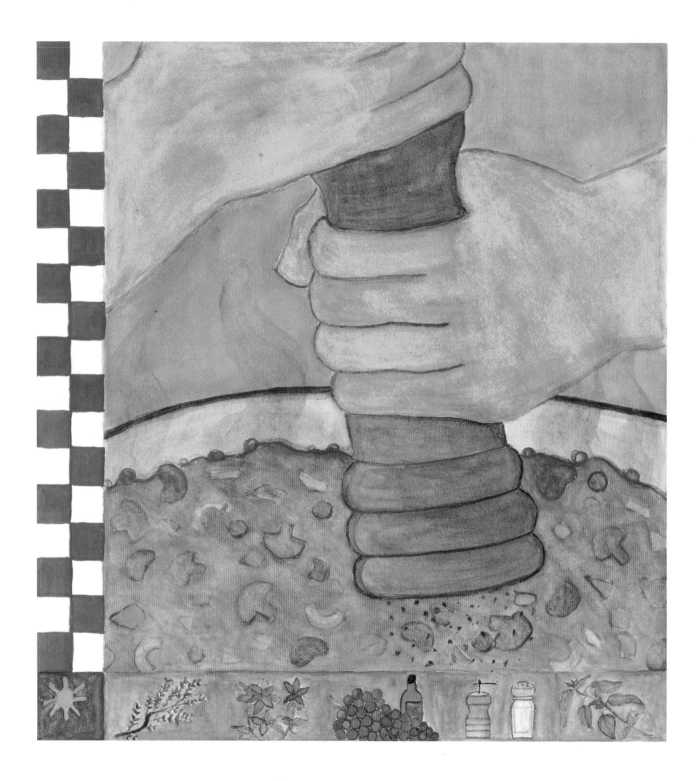

Season

Taste

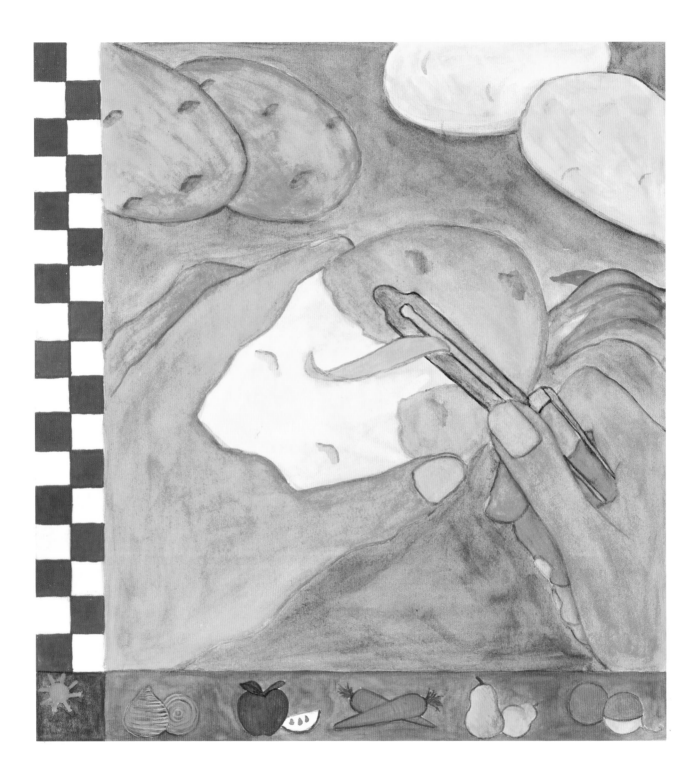

Peel

Mash

Fillet

Slice

Grill

Sauté

Toss

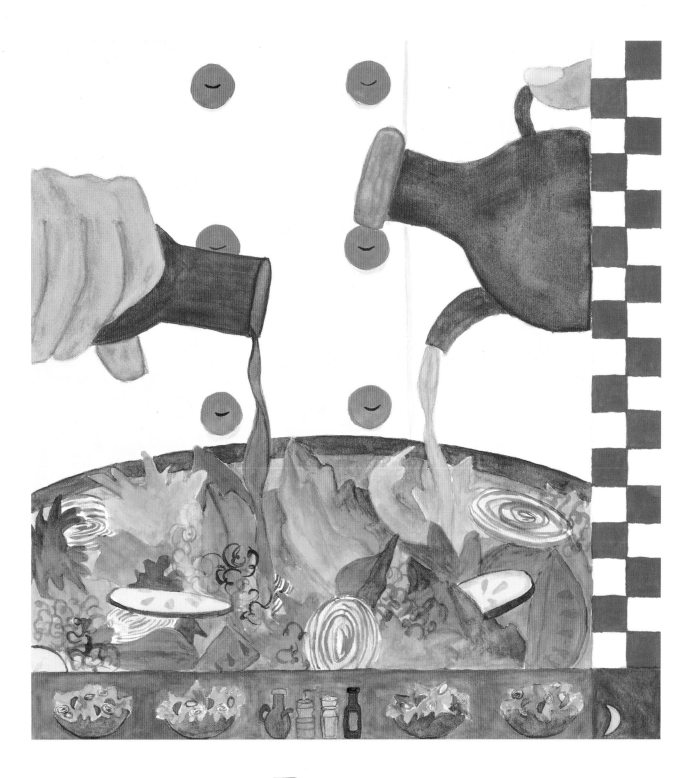

Dress

Garnish

Serve

Eat

And Eat!

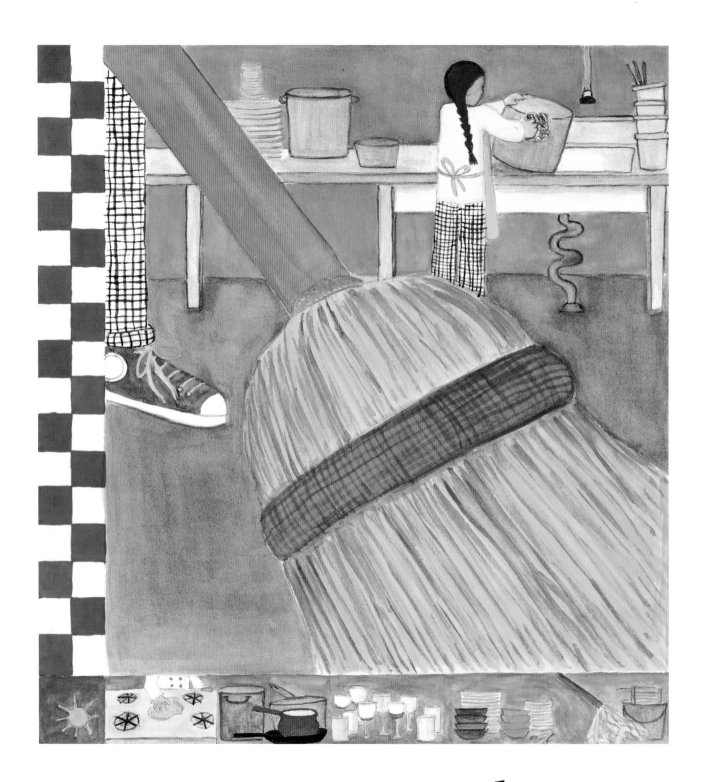

Sweep, Scrub

Yawn, Stretch